ABOUT THE AUTHOR

Originally from Surrey, Nicky now lives in Devon. She previously worked in Publishing and Direct Marketing. She has been working on her stories for several years which were inspired by her beloved Golden Retriever, Barnaby. She likes connecting with other dog lovers and enjoys writing, wine and cheese!

Goldenwood Barnaby

and his

Amazing Adventures!

Nicky Coyle

Matador
9 Priory Business Park,
Wistow Road, Kibworth Beauchamp,
Leicestershire. LE8 0RX
Tel: 0116 279 2299
Email: books@troubador.co.uk
Web: www.troubador.co.uk/matador
Twitter: @matadorbooks

ISBN 978 1838593 001

British Library Cataloguing in Publication Data.
A catalogue record for this book is available from the British Library.

Printed and bound in Great Britain by 4edge Limited
Typeset in 13pt Minion Pro by Troubador Publishing Ltd, Leicester, UK

Matador is an imprint of Troubador Publishing Ltd

With special thanks to my dear friends Frank and Debbie for becoming "The Politan Family". I hope that our boys would have been proud.

For Barnaby,

The original swishywagga,
Aug 11 2000–Sept 24 2015. Our beautiful
golden boy, forever in our hearts.

"Ask not, what your dog can do for you,
ask what you can do for your dog."

STORY ONE

BARNABY AND SPIRIT VISIT DR SORE-PAW

"Ten juicy bones sitting on the wall, ten juicy bones sitting on the wall, and if one juicy bone should accidentally fall..." Barnaby could never finish the dream. Each morning he would wake up just at the moment the bone was about to fall. Stretching and yawning, he made his way downstairs, almost resisting the temptation of the bathroom where the laundry basket was almost calling him to examine its wonderful contents and treasures. With this in mind, he picked up a sock, as it would be rude not to appear in front of anyone without a gift. The smell of bacon and buttered toast filled the air, making his nose twitch and his tummy rumble. He could hear his mum singing along to one of his favourite songs, 'Daydream Retriever', the words ringing out from the kitchen.

Barnaby walked through the kitchen and out into the garden which he called his meadow. Barnaby's mum said it should be called a mudow as Barnaby had dug lots of holes. There were three holes in particular that he was very proud of and he'd named them 'Tom, Dick and Harry' after a war film he'd seen. Maybe one day he'd be able to dig right through to the other side of the fence! The rain throughout the winter had made his meadow very muddy and the spring air was filled with the scent of the freshly cut grass and newly blossomed flowers, which sent his nose twitching for a second time. It was also a very exciting day, as his best friend Spirit was coming over to see him.

Spirit wasn't a Golden Retriever dog like Barnaby; he was what was called a Husky dog. Barnaby thought he was funny because he had trouble pronouncing the letter 'R', and that, combined with his husky voice, used to make Barnaby howl with laughter. Spirit didn't mind that Barnaby found him funny. Spirit was also an only dog and understood what it was like not to have any brothers or sisters. All they had to share things with was their humans, and each other, whenever they got together.

Barnaby had sent Spirit a fleamail three days ago, inviting him over to his house and offering to accompany him to his dogtor's appointment. He hoped he had received it safely, as fleamails could take a very long time to be delivered, depending on which carrier you used. If you used a traditional pigeon carrier it would arrive very quickly, but if you used a snail mail carrier it could take days, and sometimes if you used the latter one, they didn't get there at all. There were many theories as to why fleamails didn't arrive... One theory in particular Barnaby really didn't like to think about, and another theory involved something he'd read on the menu of a nearby restaurant... something called *l'escargot*...!

Barnaby had a quick roll on the grass and a glance through the fence to check the neighbours' cat, whom they called 'Miss Catastrophe', wasn't about. She was very quick on her paws and would sit on the fence and tease Barnaby; she could jump really high and walk along the top fence, balancing herself precisely so she wouldn't fall. Barnaby was certain she used to mutter things about him under her breath.

Barnaby's ears suddenly pricked up at the sound of the front doorbell. With a huge woof, he leapt up and ran back through the kitchen door. He stopped momentarily to consider whether he should politely eat the last remaining slice of toast and bacon, but thought maybe he shouldn't, as the pizza he had 'helped' take care of the night before was probably enough for now, and he certainly didn't want to end up in the doghouse again!

The doghouse wasn't exactly a doghouse; it was, in fact, Barnaby's bedroom. He had a lovely, soft, warm bed (not quite as comfortable as the sofa downstairs), pictures of dogs on the wall, a pile of stuffed animals, some items of underwear hidden in one corner of the room which he had 'borrowed' from the laundry basket, and an odd shoe. He did have the pair of shoes at one point but had forgotten where he had left the other one. Sometimes if he was extra naughty or if someone important was coming to visit, he would be sent to the doghouse. Seemingly, some humans didn't appreciate his wonderful way of greeting them, or that he always left the gift of golden hair on their clothes. *Most odd*, he thought, *that they in particular wouldn't like the hair, especially as most humans were completely obsessed with not having enough of it.*

He was never in the doghouse for long, though, sometimes he even played it to his advantage. He would sit facing the wall in the doghouse until his mum finally gave in and begged him to come out whilst holding a cracker and cheese as a peace offering. Racing into the lounge and almost knocking over his water bowl and narrowly missing the cord of the dreaded vacuum cleaner, he stopped at the hallway. Barnaby's mum opened the door and there stood Spirit with his human Mrs Level. She was a very tall lady, whom his mum described as being very down to earth and level-headed. Barnaby had never understood why humans liked to be level-headed, as it meant they couldn't do those cute little head tilts that most dogs do. As for being down to earth, it made much more sense to have four legs in order to be slightly above the earth.

Barnaby's mum and Mrs Level were sure to be talking for hours, so now was the perfect time for Barnaby and Spirit to go out together. Unfortunately, today's outing was to see Dr Sore-Paw. Spirit had had a funny tummy for days and Barnaby was certain it had been caused by the fact Spirit found everything hilarious. So much so that his insides hurt, almost like he'd swallowed a dozen socks. Barnaby had never done this act himself, although he'd read about it in *The Doggy Dogtor's Dictionary*, which he'd borrowed from the library and forgotten to return. Barnaby was mostly a sock stealer; indeed he had a huge collection of various socks in all different shapes, sizes, and colours. He thought some of the socks might be valuable one day.

Goldenwood is a secret world solely inhabited by dogs of various kinds, and Barnaby entered this secret world by means of an invisible dog flap at the top of his meadow. By invisible, this means it was invisible to humans, and time stood still on the human side, so on every occasion that Barnaby and his friends returned from Goldenwood, it would be exactly the same time as when they left! Spirit and Barnaby ran to the top of the meadow and Barnaby pressed his nose against the sniffer recognition system; the magic dog flap opened, whereupon both dogs walked through to the other side. Immediately they smelt the aroma of all things 'dog': muddy puddles, sandy paws, freshly baked biscuits, and grilled T-bone steaks. There was also the familiar sight of the Goldenwood Town Crier. His name was Bert and was of the British Bulldog kind, who bellowed out the words, "Oyez, oyez, welcome to Goldenwood, welcome to Goldenwood," whilst ringing his handbell with his right paw. He was magnificently dressed in a red tunic, a white shirt with a frilly lapel, long socks, heavy black shoes, and a hat with a large white feather. Barnaby didn't know much about Bert, and although he would have loved to stop and speak to him, he didn't want Spirit to be late for his dogtor's appointment.

Barnaby and Spirit started making their way along Furever Avenue – the avenue had been given that title as it was the road that went on 'forever'. The wise Great Dane dog, whose name was Pastry and who was of Danish descent, was responsible for naming Furever Avenue. Sadly, Pastry was no longer of this earth, as he passed away many years ago and had received Goldenwood's first-ever

Steak Funeral! A huge statue of Pastry had been erected and placed in the yard at St Bernard's Church, and dogs from all over the world could visit Goldenwood to see the statue and to buy miniature versions of the statue at the church gift shop, which was meant to bring good health and happiness forever to any dog who bought one. The vicar of St Bernard's, the Reverend Dawg-Collar, would donate all the money raised to help dogs who didn't have a human family. Everyone was very fond of the Reverend, as he was of the St Bernard dog kind. Big and burly, he wore a long, white cloak with a wide, black collar, and carried a small barrel of holy water under his chin. The small barrel was identical to the one St Bernard dogs used whilst rescuing people, except this barrel carried another kind of special water. The Reverend dressed this way every day, except on Sunday afternoons when you could see him informally dressed in his gardening robes and carpet slippers, tending to the church flowers and plants. He also had a huge vegetable patch and would give the produce to his congregation every Sunday morning.

After a walk of about five minutes, Barnaby and Spirit arrived at Dr Sore-Paw's surgery. The surgery was situated off Furever Avenue in a little cul-de-sac called Medicinal Mews. All the buildings looked the same, except for Dr Sore-Paws surgery, which was painted in a powder-blue colour and had a big brass plaque that read 'Dr Ivor Sore-Paw, Medical Dogtor'. Underneath the plaque were a lot of large letters such as MD, BMA, BSc, PhD. Barnaby thought Dr Sore-Paw must be very smart to have all those letters after his name.

Most dogs found it scary the first time they saw Dr Sore-Paw, although after meeting him they always felt better. Barnaby nudged open the door to various dogs of all different kinds waiting to be examined by the dogtor. Barnaby caught a glimpse of a particular lady dog whom he really didn't want to meet. "Oh no," he whispered to Spirit. "That's Mrs Fussy-Paws." She was of the Yorkshire Terrier dog kind and always wore designer dog coats, a necklace and diamond collar, and her claws were always painted red. She was so short she had trouble seeing a lot of the other dogs who were waiting in the surgery. However, she had eyes like a wolf on a full moon and a voice to match. She quite literally never stopped talking! Her first name was 'Joyce' and it was rumoured her neighbours called her 'Joyce the Voice', as she was such a gossip. She also had a very annoying, shrill bark and Barnaby thought it amusing that such a small, delicate-looking dog could be so loud. Barnaby continued whispering to Spirit, "If she sees us, every dog in Goldenwood will know why we're here, let's sit around the corner!"

Dr Sore-Paw's receptionist, Mrs Sore-Paw, walked over to welcome them. She was very different to her husband, her being the Poodle dog kind, with beautiful, tight, curly, white hair and a pink ribbon around her neck. She was dressed in a pale pink and grey twinset with a chunky gold wrist watch, and she always smelled of 'Poochie', the latest fragrance which all the famous celebrity lady dogs were wearing. She suggested they help themselves to a magazine while they waited. Their favourite magazine was *Wagga's Weekly*, which was filled with all the latest doggy news, including famous pup stars, new fashion accessories and doggoscopes. Barnaby picked up the magazine, as he liked to read his doggoscope which predicted his future. It read, "Leo: You may have to play Cupid, as a good friend is about to find love. It's also a good week for new adventures." A double-page pull-out poster was in the magazine every week, which featured a different famous dog actor or actress. The poster inside this issue of the magazine was missing. Barnaby was disappointed, because the poster was of the famous actress 'Deanna Dachshund'. The magazine also had a problem page which had helped many dogs through difficult times and Barnaby was proud because he had helped create it. A few minutes passed and Mrs Sore-Paw called Spirit's name out loudly: "Spirit Level to Dr Sore-Paw's office, please!"

"Would you like me to come in with you and hold your paw, Spirit?" said Barnaby quietly, so as not to cause him embarrassment. Spirit nodded and they both made their way through to the dogtor's office.

Dr Sore-Paw was of the Japanese Akita dog kind; he had a strong accent and wore little round dark-rimmed glasses which sat at the bottom of his nose. He was dressed in a pinstriped suit, wore a tie round his neck, and had an article hanging over his broad chest that looked somewhat like an old-fashioned dog lead. Barnaby had discovered that article was called a stethoscope and all dogtors wore them. Dr Sore-Paw was very old-fashioned and sometimes would forget the English language and write his prescriptions in Japanese, which Mrs Sore-Paw would have to translate. It was fortunate Mrs Sore-Paw had studied in Japan as a puppy and had learned to speak and write the language well.

Spirit explained about his tummy symptoms and Dr Sore-Paw gently examined him. "Well, Spirit," he said, "I can only put this down to too much laughing. Laughing, of course, in moderation is good for you, but it can hurt your insides after a while. I've even heard of many a human saying they've laughed so much it hurt. It is my professional opinion, and I would confidently state, you have a bad case of 'LAPDOG', commonly known as 'Laughter and Puppy Dog Overexcited Gastrics'!"

Barnaby laughed at the diagnosis, as he had arrived at this conclusion much earlier. Spirit had to try very hard not to laugh again. "I'll give you a prescription for some medicine and you must refrain from laughing for at least two hours or it won't be effective. There is also the chance in extreme cases where you end up with an upset tummy if you miss a dose or take too much medicine." Spirit thanked Dr Sore-Paw, and he and Barnaby walked back to the reception area where Mrs Sore-Paw thanked them for coming and gave both dogs a treat. As they were about to leave, they heard a shrill, earth-shattering voice: "Good morning, Barnaby, good morning, Spirit, just a routine visit and nothing serious, I hope?"

"Quick," said Barnaby, "Joyce Fussy-Paws has seen us, let's get going before she comes over!"

"Do you think we have time to pop into The Collar and Leash Cafe for a quick snack?" said Barnaby.

Spirit nodded in agreement. "But what if Mrs Fussy-Paws comes in and sees us, Bawnaby?" exclaimed Spirit.

"She won't go in there, Spirit," said Barnaby. "Her chauffeur was waiting for her outside the surgery and she never goes anywhere unaccompanied. She always has to have someone to hold her handbag or umbrella up in the rain, plus she frequents the more expensive restaurants, and anyway, she's not even a foot tall. I doubt she could even see above the table as she looks down her snout at everyone."

"You're vewy funny, Bawnaby!" chuckled Spirit.

They entered the cafe and sat down at a table, which was beautifully arranged with a red check tablecloth and bone china teacups, which by luck were shaped like real bones. There was also little sachets of jam and butter, and a large pot of cream. They ordered traditional English scones with a pot of tea. The waitress was a very pretty lady of the Red Setter dog kind; she had beautiful, long, deep red, shiny fur and resembled the season autumn in a colour. She was wearing a pretty apron with the letters 'C & L' printed on it in entwined gold italics, and she wore a badge with the name 'Cecilia'. Spirit blushed as the waitress placed the teapot on the table; he just couldn't believe how beautiful she was!

"These scones are lovely," said Barnaby, "but not as good as Mum's, talking of which, we should be getting back now."

"Can't we stay faw just one mowe cup of tea?" Spirit replied, looking in the direction of the pretty waitress.

Barnaby smiled at Spirit. "You like her, don't you? But we must get going, we can come back soon!"

Spirit blushed with embarrassment and almost ran to the door, hoping that the waitress wouldn't notice. Just as he was about to open the door, he heard a voice behind him. "Excuse me, you're Spirit, aren't you?" It was the waitress, standing right behind Spirit.

"Yes, I am," he replied in a rather embarrassed manner.

"I'm Cecilia, but you can call me CC for short. I thought you might like this slice of cake to take home with you," she said rather confidently.

"Thank you vewy much," replied Spirit.

"You're welcome, see you later, Spirit," said the waitress. Spirit certainly would look forward to going back to the cafe and hopefully very soon! Spirit stood still for a minute, thinking how CC knew his name... and why did she want him to call her 'CC for Short', why not just CC?

They walked back up Furever Avenue, a little slower this time due to full tummies. They made one stop at the pharmacy, which was called 'Remy-D's', to get Spirit's medicine. Barnaby always liked going there, as it had a big sign over the shop doorway that read 'Remy-D's Apothecary and Fine Home Remedies Since 1896'. It didn't just dispense medicines, it also sold many things, including toilet soaps, bath salts, hot water bottles and all sorts of home remedies that had been in the D'ispenser family for years, along with something named travel sweets arranged in little round tins.

Barnaby's mum had travel sweets in what she called the glovebox in the car. Barnaby very much wanted to see the contents of the glovebox, but it was strictly off limits since the time he'd eaten two of the fingers off her favourite pair. The shop was a family concern and had originally been run by Mr D'ispenser Senior of the Italian Spinone dog kind. He emigrated over from Italy with his family many years ago, but now his great-great-grandson Remy Junior was in charge. It was rumoured that Mr D Senior was still alive and lived above the shop, although he hadn't been seen for years. Barnaby thought if he was still alive, he'd be well into his hundreds (in dog years) by now. Fortunately Spirit's prescription had been written in English and this made prescribing the medicine easier, so they were soon on their way back home. There are many other sites shops and places to visit along Furever Avenue and in Goldenwood in general, but they will have to wait for another time.

They arrived home and entered through the magic dog flap into Barnaby's meadow. The sun was shining and everything was just as it was. Time had stood still: the socks and stuffed animals on the lawn, a punctured football, and a paddling pool still full of water.

"We'd better wash our paws, Spirit," said Barnaby. "You know how Mum is so house-proud, if we don't wash our paws, she will switch on the vacuum cleaner, and you know how much I hate that horrible machine. Sometimes I've actually seen it move by itself, it's more scarier than when Miss Catastrophe fights with the other felines in the middle of the night! Mum even sings and dances with it sometimes, although I've never worked out why."

Barnaby's mum and Mrs Level were sitting in the kitchen talking. Unfortunately the plate of biscuits was empty, as was the coffee pot. *Shame about the biscuits*, thought Barnaby, but not the coffee, as coffee made Barnaby cough. He thought maybe the humans had misspelled coffee as it should definitely be called 'coughy'. He'd found that out a couple of years ago when he'd helped himself to a cup that had been left next to his mum's chair. He'd almost nearly ended up going to visit Dr Sore-Paw but decided against it when he saw a TV programme about forbidden foods for dogs. He still found it difficult to fathom that any foods could be forbidden, but the coffee had convinced him otherwise.

"Thank you faw coming with me today," said Spirit.

"You're welcome," smiled Barnaby. "Just make sure you take the medicine correctly as Dr Sore-Paw told you, we don't want you to get another funny tummy!"

Both dogs walked back into the house and sat at the feet of their respective humans. *If only they knew about Goldenwood*, thought Barnaby, *or maybe it's best they don't!*

Another adventure for Barnaby was to be had the next day, when he was to visit a very special royal friend of his. He couldn't wait, but for now he would go back to dreaming about his juicy bones sitting on the wall; maybe he might even get to the end of his dream tomorrow!

STORY TWO

BARNABY GOES TO BARKINGHAM PALACE!

Dawn broke as Barnaby awoke from his usual dream. He didn't know Dawn or why she was broken; maybe he'd find out one day. Stretching and yawning, he made his way downstairs. The usual familiar smell of bacon and toast was filling the air – or wait, maybe today it was sausages. The radio was playing another golden favourite tune, 'Man I Feel Like a Golden', the words echoing against the kitchen tiles.

Dropping the mail on the kitchen floor that he'd so thoughtfully pulled through the letterbox, Barnaby made his way up his meadow and through the magic dog flap. Today he was going to visit his dear friend Dut-Chess. She lived at Barkingham Palace and he had originally planned to take Spirit along for the walk, but Spirit had finally plucked up the courage to ask CC (or CC for Short, as she'd affectionately become known), out on a date. Therefore, on this occasion, Barnaby decided to go by himself.

Barkingham Palace was situated right at the top of Goldenwood Hills; it was a beautiful building with a little bridge leading to the entrance and had a moat around the outside with ducks and swans swimming in the water. Dut-Chess had originally lived there with her parents and grandparents, but now she lived alone with a household of other animals. Barnaby often thought that she was like 'Audrey Forbes-Hamilton', a character from an old 1970's show that his mum had watched when she was a pup!

She had two of everything and because of this she had earned the name of Double-Dutch. Dut-Chess was of the Bloodhound dog kind and she was always well turned out, often wearing a tweed skirt with a matching blouse, a headscarf, and tall, leather, walking boots. She was what was called 'Terribly Awfully', and very well-spoken. The thing Barnaby liked about her most was that she was a fabulous chess player and Barnaby's pet name for her was 'Dut-Chess'! She had won numerous competitions, both in Goldenwood and overseas. Barnaby had only beaten her once, and that was only when she'd been distracted by her two tortoises named Turtleneck and Sweater, who had gone missing. They eventually turned up three weeks later outside Mr Chip-Olatas Butcher's Shop. They had looked a bit worse for wear and someone had jokingly written the words 'This way up' in chalk on their shells. They had also been sandwiched between some steak pie boxes and had a very lucky escape, but dear old Chip had kindly returned them to Dut-Chess before they could get into any more trouble!

Barnaby walked up Furever Avenue, taking a shortcut through the churchyard and out into Hairpin Lane. He stopped to speak to Henrietta Foreclaw-Kennelworth, who ran a charming little farm shop. She had chickens roaming around, trugs full of fresh vegetables, eggs, and flower arrangements. Henrietta was of the St Bernard dog kind like the Reverend Dawg-Collar, and they were, in fact, cousins. Henrietta Foreclaw had married Henry Kennelworth forty years ago and they had two grown-up pups who no longer lived with them, but the shop and cottage behind it still looked like a proper family concern. Everyone referred to them as 'the H's' on account of the fact that they were both called Henry.

Henrietta asked Barnaby if he wouldn't mind taking some eggs and herbs up to the Palace as Dut-Chess was planning a summer ball. Her servants normally came down to collect such things, but old Mr Tail Feather, the head housekeeper, had a very bad cold and had passed it on to several of the staff, so he had sent them to their kennels for total bedrest.

Barnaby waved goodbye to Henrietta and made his way to Barkingham Palace. Walking across the wooden bridge, he smiled at the mother duck and her ducklings swimming happily underneath. For a short moment he had a picture in his head of pancakes and hoisin sauce, but he quickly put those thoughts out of his mind!

Barnaby leant forward, pressing his nose on the big, round doorbell. He could hear it ringing out the tune of 'Who Let the Dogs Out'. This always made him laugh as Dut-Chess had replaced the original doorbell that played the music of 'Land of Hope and Glory', as in her opinion the tune was out of date and not representative of the Modern Doggy Monarchy.

"Barnaby, daaarling," Dut-Chess exclaimed in a loud voice. "How lovely to see you, please come in and have a seat to take the weight off your paws."

Barnaby walked into the large reception room and sat down. The table had been laid with a fresh pot of tea and a vast array of cakes on a tower-like stand. On the other side of the table was the magnificent chessboard, with all of its pieces hand-carved and varnished. Rather than kings and queens, pawns, knights, bishops, and rooks, these chess pieces represented different dog breeds and was a sight to behold.

As they sat down to play chess, Dut-Chess enquired if Barnaby would like to come to her summer ball on Saturday night, as she had invited a few other friends and was in the process of organising some live music for the event. Dut-Chess also asked if Barnaby could arrange for Singapaw-Sam to be the main act at the ball. She also wanted to invite Spirit and his new girlfriend, the pretty young waitress from The Collar and Leash Cafe.

"No problem on both things," replied Barnaby. "I'll fleamail them both later."

Singapaw-Sam was a fantastic singer and could turn his paw to most musical instruments. He was of the Akita dog kind like Dr Sore-Paw, but they weren't related. He was very tall and wore a midnight-blue suit with a black-and-white pattern tie which looked like piano keys, and black shiny shoes. He was an excellent dancer and sometimes would invite the girl dogs up on stage to dance with him during his act.

After a fantastic game of chess, which ended three hours later thanks to a checkmate from Dut-Chess, Barnaby made his way back home. At seven o'clock on Saturday evening two days later he got dressed up for his return visit to Barkingham Palace. He looked in the mirror and was impressed with his appearance. He had had a bath, and his blond, wavy coat was soft and shiny; he was wearing his best dinner suit, complete with bow tie and a starched, white shirt. He had also sprayed himself with the latest canine fragrance called 'Gold Magnet'. "If only Cousin Cosmo could see me now!" he exclaimed.

Barnaby arrived at Barkingham Palace promptly at 8.30pm and was shown into the magnificent ballroom. The ballroom had crystal chandeliers hanging from the ceiling and the mix of light and crystal from the chandeliers lit up the room. The dinner table was full of shiny gold cutlery with crystal glasses and little bone-shaped name placecards. Dut-Chess appeared and looked magnificent in her red ballgown with pearl earrings and a matching tiara. As the ballroom began filling up, Barnaby caught sight of Spirit with CC for Short, who looked stunning in a white gown and garnet necklace which matched her flame-red hair.

Bert the Town Crier had been hired by Dut-Chess to announce dinner. "Dinner is served," he shouted in a very forthright and robust manner. As everyone took their places for dinner, a vast array of wonderful meaty delights arrived. Prime Aberdeen Angus steak (courtesy of Mr Chip-Olata's cousin Angus), chicken breasts wrapped in smoky bacon, barbecue pork ribs, beef wellington in a red wine sauce, which had actually been served in one of Dut-Chess's old wellington boots. As Dut-Chess rose to her feet to make a toast, she tapped her glass with a thick, warm, brown slice of bread and exclaimed loudly, "To all of us, and to good health, wealth, and happiness!"

After dinner, the guests made their way to the top end of the ballroom. Singapaw-Sam had his band set up on the raised platform, which almost resembled a proper stage. The dinner table had been cleared away and several other tables and chairs had been placed around the floor of the ballroom. As Singapaw-Sam began his first song, several doggy couples made their way to the floor. Spirit and CC for Short, the Reverend and Mrs Dawg-Collar, Mr and Mrs Foreclaw-Kennelworth and two single lady dogs, Dilly and Dally Dachshund. They were sisters and had never married. They had arrived from Germany several years ago and were of the Dachshund dog kind, just like their surname. The sisters were always together and owned and ran a milliner's shop in Furever Avenue named 'Herr Loss Hats'. All the hats were paw-made on the premises and, although expensive, were beautifully designed to suit each individual customer. Barnaby laughed at the sisters, as they were wearing raised paw shoes to make them appear taller! They were great dancers and their long, slender bodies moved perfectly in time with the music. The party was now in full swing and Dut-Chess stood in the middle of the dance floor 'voguing' like the human pop star Madonna, which gave the guests much delight.

All of a sudden there was a loud knock at the front door; it was so loud you could hear it above the music playing in the ballroom. Dut-Chess walked through to the hallway, muttering under her breath about some very late guests, when the front door flew open. Standing dressed in a scarlet-red ballgown with matching shoes and tiara was a dog, of the same kind as Dut-Chess; she wasn't unlike her facially except she was shorter and heavier set.

"Well, well, well, if it isn't Luci-Fur," said Dut-Chess. "You were the last dog I was expecting to see here tonight!"

Luci-Fur was the sister of Dut-Chess and had fallen out many years previously when she had stolen the collection of jewels which had been in the family for generations. "So nice to see you again, Sis," Luci-Fur said in a polite, kind tone. "I just had to come and see you and say how sorry I am for my actions, I can't believe how appallingly I behaved, will you please forgive me?"

By this time, many of the other guests had started to gather in the front reception hall, where there was a strange, eerie silence. Dut-Chess cleared her throat. "How could you ever expect me to forgive you after you brought such shame and disgrace to the family?"

It was at that moment Luci-Fur did the one thing that any dog in Goldenwood was forbidden to do. She sat down on her back legs, raised her front paws up and went into a full beg! No dog was ever to beg for anything or anyone, including humans, except in very extreme circumstances.

"Well," said Dut-Chess. "You have taken the lowest possible step and decided to beg to me, Luci. If, and only if, I decide to allow you back into my home, I will expect you to contribute to the maintenance and management of Barkingham Palace. Dog knows, you could do with some exercise, as you have the behind of a Golden Retriever. Sorry, Barnaby, daaarling," Dut-Chess exclaimed. "No offence meant. There will also be no special privileges, no hunting, no spa treatments and definitely no designer clothing or jewellery."

Luci gulped, almost as if she were about to spit out a huge furball and the colour drained from her face. Her eyes started to glaze over with the shock of what her sister had just said. "For goodness' sake, girl," Dut-Chess said. "Get up from begging before you contract arthritis in your hind legs. Go to the servant's kennels and bed down there for tonight. I'll see you tomorrow at breakfast!"

Dut-Chess turned on her heels, clicked her front right paw, and cheerily told everyone to return to the ballroom and carry on with the party. The guests carried on dancing, but the atmosphere had changed. They did, however, finish off the evening with a long doggy conga. The line of dogs made its way out of the Palace and into the grounds, paws flying everywhere. It had been a marvellous evening and Luci had certainly made an entrance and was sure to be the talk of Goldenwood for some time!

Barnaby and several other guests had been invited to stay overnight at the Palace; Barnaby was fortunate to have been given the Royal Pedigree Suite. It was a magnificent bedroom, beautifully decorated with a large, four-poster bed, and a goose and duck down duvet with fluffy pillows. In one corner was an area with a huge drinking fountain and treat selection. Next to that was a chaise lounge, a television, and a table with various magazines, books, beautifully embossed writing paper, and an old-fashioned ink fountain pen. Barnaby noticed a small metal box on the sideboard and recognised it as the voice-activated Smart Bark System. He didn't realise the Smart Bark System was available in Goldenwood, although his cousin Cosmo, who lived in another country, had the same system. The system worked by either barking or speaking into it and it would obey your command.

"OK, Dougal," Barnaby said. "Play me a song by The Corgis." Instantly it began to play one of their songs, 'Every Dog's Gotta Learn Sometime'. Next to the four-poster bed was a huge bathroom with a walk-in shower, jacuzzi, and a very discreet dog bidet. Barnaby awoke in the morning after a comfortable sleep in the four-poster bed and began to eat his breakfast, which Dut-Chess had kindly provided. The large breakfast consisted of Lincolnshire sausages, smoked bacon, poached eggs, potato cakes, black pudding, and a side of hot buttered toast, fruit juice, and a large pot of tea, all served on a gleaming silver tray.

After breakfast, with a full tummy, Barnaby dressed himself in his hunting outfit, complete with cap and leather boots. He didn't hunt often and wasn't the quickest at retrieving, and sometimes he dropped the ducks and other game birds as he felt sorry for them, but he enjoyed the exercise, fresh air, and the company of his friends.

Luci-Fur hadn't been since last night, although Spirit had said he'd seen her in the drawing room with Dut-Chess shortly after breakfast. Everyone hoped the sisters would reconcile their differences and both turn over a new leaf. Barnaby had no idea what that saying meant, as he had turned over lots of times and indeed rolled over in many leaves over the years. After returning from his hunting trip and devouring a hearty Sunday lunch of roast beef and Yorkshire pudding with all the trimmings, Barnaby went to his room to pack his overnight bag and then went downstairs to express his thanks and goodbyes to Dut-Chess and the other guests.

Spirit and CC for Short were waiting in the downstairs hallway. CC was meeting a friend for a tennis match, so Barnaby and Spirit decided to walk home slowly and maybe do a little shopping at Furever Avenue. Many of the shops were now open seven days a week, with the exception of Mr Chip-Olatas Butcher's Shop, Remy D's and The Hair of the Dog Barber's Shop, who were very old-fashioned and traditional and refused to open on Sunday, as it was considered a day of rest. Barnaby and Spirit discussed various things whilst walking, including Luci-Fur, what an enjoyable evening it had been, and, in particular, when Singapaw-Sam performed a rather enthusiastic dance move and ripped his trousers open, which left him very red-faced and embarrassed.

Back at the Palace, Dut-Chess and Luci had spent the afternoon going through more of the house rules. The rules had been neatly typed on Barkingham Palace letterheaded notepaper and Luci had to sign her pawtograph and agree to them all.

The list of rules read as follows:

1. Miss Luci-Fur Snifter-Tipple is not to leave the grounds of Barkingham Palace for a period of six months from this date.

2. Miss Luci-Fur Snifter-Tipple is not permitted to attend any social events arranged by any member of the family or resident of the Goldenwood community.

3. Miss Luci-Fur Snifter-Tipple is not permitted to purchase any items other than what is absolutely essential for canine health and vitality.

4. Miss Luci-Fur Snifter-Tipple is not permitted to consume any food or intoxicating drinks other than what has been prepared by the servants of Barkingham Palace.

5. Miss Luci-Fur Snifter-Tipple is not permitted to visit any health spa or groomers without written prior permission.
6. Miss Luci-Fur Snifter-Tipple must assist the servants and groundsman of Barkingham Palace between the hours of 7am and 7pm Monday to Saturday with only one rest day per week.

Dut-Chess had placed particular emphasis on rule four, as Luci had in the past been known to be regularly intoxicated until the early hours of the morning! Luci had reluctantly agreed to all the rules, as she knew she would never receive the forgiveness of her older sister if she disagreed. She was also truly repentant for what had happened in the past.

Back in Furever Avenue, Barnaby and Spirit continued their walk home; the late afternoon sun was warm and there was a scent of BBQs in the air. They stopped at The Full Bowl Pub for a drink and sat in the beer garden reading the Sunday papers. Both dogs looked up simultaneously when they read who was on the front page. "How on earth did the *The Goldenwood Observer* know about this so quickly?!" exclaimed Barnaby. On the front page, staring right at them, was a photo of Luci-Fur taken at the Palace, with the headline above which read 'DOUBLE-DUTCH SHUNS SISTER AT SUMMER BALL EXTRAVAGANZA'.

Dut-Chess was sitting in her sun lounge as the remainder of the guests had all departed. She was tired and her paws ached from all the dance moves the night before. She poured herself a fresh cup of tea and lifted one newspaper off the stack on the coffee table and read the headlines, the same headlines Barnaby and Spirit had read. "Oh my dog," she said quietly under her breath. "'The Pupparazzi' were here last night and I never noticed or invited them." Dut-Chess wasn't easily shocked, but one thing she hated was anyone or anything bringing shame on the family. After some consideration, she felt that maybe it was better that everything was now out in the open.

Luci had seemed genuinely sorry for what had happened. *And everyone deserves a second chance in life*, she thought. Luci hadn't been the same since her husband had left her and run off with the sister of Joyce Fussy-Paws. He had taken all her money, her favourite rings, and the necklace which her late mother had left her. She was destitute and had often spent nights sleeping in Goldenwood Park, and occasionally at the Homeless Dogs Sanctuary.

Barnaby and Spirit finished their drinks at The Full Bowl Pub and carried on with their walking. The sun was setting and the air was cooler. They could hear the bells ringing at St Bernard's Church calling those who wanted to attend the evening service. Barnaby wasn't particularly religious, but today he and Spirit had thought it might be a nice way to end the day to attend the service. The church congregation was small, but the hymns were rousing and the Reverend Dawg-Collar said a prayer for Luci-Fur. The service ended with the usual prayer:

"Our dog who art in Devon, Pastry be his name. Thy kingdom come, thy will be done on earth as it is in Devon. Give us this day our daily bone and forgive us our trespasses, as we forgive those who trespass against us and lead us not into temptation but deliver us from seagulls, adog."

Whilst leaving the church, Barnaby and Spirit placed some coins in the church collection box and exchanged a few words with the Reverend Dawg-Collar. Mrs Dawg-Collar handed them both a basket of freshly picked vegetables, "For your mothers," she said cheerily, followed by, "don't leave it as long to attend church next time, you two, remember, Dog is watching you both and it's always nice to see you both in church!"

"Thank you very much for the vegetables and for your advice," said Barnaby. They then walked through the churchyard and up the remainder of Furever Avenue.

At the top of Furever Avenue, Barnaby and Spirit walked through the magic dog flap and back into Barnaby's meadow. Time had stood still as always, and just like after any other trip to Goldenwood, everything was just as he'd left it. Barnaby smiled at the thought that he had a second dinner to look forward to later. Spirit said goodbye and made his way home, and Barnaby walked into the lounge and sat next to his mum.

Another adventure was to be had tomorrow when Barnaby's relatives, the Politan family, were visiting!

STORY THREE

BARNABY MEETS THE POLITAN FAMILY!

Barnaby woke up from his usual dream to the sound of his iBone ringing. He had set the alarm for 7am as he was so excited about his cousin Cosmo visiting with his parents today. He stretched, yawned, and made his way downstairs, the usual smell of breakfast meeting his nose and another golden favourite playing on the radio. It was a cover version of a song by The Mummas and The Daddys or something like that.

Cosmo, his mum Metro, and his dad Neo were arriving at around noon. Barnaby wanted everything to be just perfect for Cosmo as he would be sharing his room. His mum had washed his bedding and made up a spare bed, she had even washed all his stuffed animals – much to his annoyance, as he knew that they wouldn't smell the same as before. Who on earth would want a stuffed animal that smelt of lavender? The house was sparkly clean; even most of Barnaby's fur had been vacuumed up and all his toys had been placed in his toy chest. There were no loose undergarments or socks to be seen anywhere, either. Most of all, though, Barnaby was so excited to be able to take Cosmo to Goldenwood. Cosmo had never been, partly because he lived many miles away in a country called America and you had to cross a big pond to get there. Barnaby liked ponds; they were always filled with interesting things and they made you smell nice.

Right on the dot of noon, the front doorbell rang. Barnaby barked with delight and pushed past his mum to answer the door. "Will you ever learn some manners?" she said in quite a stern tone. There standing in the doorway was Cosmo with Mr and Mrs Politan. Barnaby's mum hugged

Metro Politan, Cosmo's mum, and Neo Politan, Cosmo's dad, and then bent down to cuddle Cosmo. What she wasn't expecting was that he had a condition called 'Excessive Greeting Disorder'. Barnaby had it too; it was in the family history. Just at the minute Barnaby's mum bent down, Cosmo launched himself at her, pushing her back onto the hall carpet, her legs flying into the air. His front paws rested on her shoulders, washing her face at the same time! Neo grabbed Cosmo by his collar and apologised profusely. Barnaby chuckled; what an entrance Cosmo had made!

The two dogs were quickly led outside to the garden. "Howdy, Cous," said Cosmo with his heavy American accent. He was so much like Barnaby to look at it was uncanny; they could certainly have been brothers. He had the same colouring and beautiful swishy tail. The only difference was that Barnaby was slightly stockier and had what they called a blocky head. The two dogs did several laps of the garden in celebration of seeing one another, refreshing themselves with a large bowl of water afterwards.

"I sure can't wait to see Goldenwood," said Cosmo. "I've been telling all my dawgie friends about this here visit and I'm so excited, which reminds me," he continued, "I need to buy some of those miniature statues of the Great Dane Pastry, everyone back home wants one!"

"OK, then, let's not waste another minute, we'll go now!" Barnaby exclaimed joyously. "Just push your nose against the dog flap, Cosmo, I've already programmed your nose print into the sniffer recognition system."

"Yee-haw!" exclaimed Cosmo, who placed his nose against the flap and magically it opened. He walked through, followed closely by Barnaby.

"Oyez, oyez, good morning, gentlemen, and a very warm welcome to Goldenwood," said Bert the Town Crier. Cosmo's face lit up with sheer delight at the sight before him; it wasn't just the sight of Bert that made him smile but the smell that went rippling through his nostrils. He had read about it many times but had never imagined that it would be as nice as this!

The two dogs started to walk down Furever Avenue, stopping briefly to ask the Reverend Dawg-Collar for twelve miniature Pastry statues that they would collect on their way home later. Barnaby pulled a piece of paper from under his collar; it was a list of things that he thought

Cosmo might like to do whilst in Goldenwood. First on the list was a spot of lunch at The Full Bowl Pub, the same place he had stopped at before with Spirit.

Cosmo had always wanted to go to a traditional pub. He'd been to places in America that were called dog friendly bars, but they weren't anything like this. From the outside it looked like a thatched cottage, like a picture on one those traditional English postcards. It had a small, stable-like door and inside, very low ceilings. There were big, wooden tables and seats with wide cushions, and something that Cosmo had never seen before called a dart board. It was fixed to a wall in the corner and two dogs called Jack and Russell, who worked at The Hair of the Dog Barber's Shop, were throwing bone-shaped things at it.

"I say, Barnaby, I have never seen anything like that in my life before, or indeed like that," said Cosmo, pointing to Dilly and Dally Daschund, who were playing dominoes and drinking beer out of tall glasses!

Then all of a sudden one of the dogs playing darts shouted, "One hundred and eighty!" Barnaby explained that meant they had hit the top score. Cosmo spotted the fruit machine in the corner; he had seen these on TV before but could never work out why there wasn't any actual fruit in it. This one was a dog version, though. He put some coins into the slot and pressed the big red button to start the game; he needed to match three dog leads for a prize or, even better, three bones for the jackpot. The lights on the machine started flashing, along with some funny sounds. Unfortunately, Cosmo didn't win anything this time, and he didn't want to put too much money in; he'd enjoyed playing with it, though.

Barnaby and Cosmo sat overlooking the garden and ate a hearty ploughman's lunch washed down with a fizzy cola drink. Cosmo said he missed that, even though he'd only been away from home a couple days.

Next on the list was supposed to be a visit to Barkingham Palace, but Barnaby had explained what had happened at the ball and that it wasn't a good idea right now. The third thing on the list was that Cosmo had wanted to take a rowing boat out on the River Gold. Cosmo knew all about the Great Lakes back home, but he'd always wanted to row a boat using the oars properly by himself. Barnaby reached into his Wag for Life (his mum had one of these bags too, but for some reason she called it a Bag for Life) and handed Cosmo a gift he'd bought him from Herr Loss Hats, Dilly and Dally milliner's shop. Inside was a fabulous straw boater hat and Cosmo put it on; he looked dashing!

They paid the boating lake attendant for their hour and set off on their way, joyously singing, "Row, row row your boat gently down the stream, merrily merrily, merrily, merrily, Goldenwood's a dream!", followed by another rather enthusiastic, "Yee-haw!" from Cosmo.

This turned the heads of two lady dogs rowing ahead of them, to which Cosmo raised his hat and said, "Good afternoon, ladies, and what a mighty fine one it is too!" Barnaby took his turn at the oars and off they went, laughing and joking together. One joke really tickled Cosmo, as Barnaby told him it: "Did you hear the one about the pup who swallowed a 50p coin? Well, the dogtor visited him and asked his mother how he was and she replied, 'Sorry, Dogtor, there's still no change!'"

An hour later, they returned to the boathouse. They had enjoyed the trip so very much. Cosmo had been disappointed that he couldn't visit

Barkingham Palace, but Barnaby had come up with an idea: the Palace may not have been open today but the Barkingham Maze would be. Barnaby was fascinated by the maze; his mum had told him about the human version at a place near London called Hampton Court. The maze was very similar to that – except it was a doggy version, of course – so rather than just work your way from one corner and find your way out, you had to use your nose and sniff your way out. At the end every dog received some treats in a box with a picture of Barkingham Palace on it. Rumour had it that one time Joyce Fussy-Paws and her friend had got so lost they had to wait for one of the Barkingham Palace Groundsmen to find them the next morning! Seemingly Joyce had barked very loudly but the groundsman had rather bad selective deafness, or at least that's what he had told everyone. To this day, Joyce had never gone back there and she avoided talking about the experience altogether!

Cosmo was happy to go to the maze; he'd also get to see the grounds of Barkingham Palace while he was there. Both dogs made their way up Hair Pin Lane and crossed the wooden footbridge at the rear of the Palace. There were lots of other dogs visiting with their young pups who all seemed be having a great time. There were also some doggy morris dancers performing their routine. Cosmo was intrigued by these weirdly dressed dogs waving their poles, jingling away in time with one another. "Here we are, Cous," said Barnaby. "We start here and just follow the trail with our noses, I think."

Noses to the ground, they started along the pathway divided by neatly trimmed, tall, green hedges. Several times they thought that they had made it out, only to find a dead end, or even finding themselves back at the entrance again. Barnaby started to panic at one point as his iBone had a very low battery and he was worried that he wouldn't be able to call for help if they weren't able to find their way out. After about three quarters of an hour they eventually managed to find their way through to the other side. Cosmo looked at Barnaby, who still looked a little panicked and said, "I say, Cous, you were looking a little scared there for a while, I think that you thought we were going to end up barking for help like that Joyce Fussy-Paws!"

Barnaby blushed with embarrassment. "I have to go to the little dogs' room, Cosmo," Barnaby replied, visibly shaken by the whole experience. Cosmo had never seen Barnaby move so quickly! He picked their bags of treats up; one of the Groundsmen very kindly gave him a few extra boxes to take home as souvenirs.

There was one last thing to do today before heading home and that was to visit the Gentleman's Outfitters in Furever Avenue called 'Tailor Made'. Tobias Tailor was of the Afghan Hound dog kind; he was extremely tall and wiry, with very long, sleek hair and he always wore a black suit, with a white shirt and waistcoat. He always had a tape measure around his neck, although he had a wonderful talent of being able to tell every dog's exact measurements just by looking at them. Barnaby and Cosmo walked into the shop, where everything was arranged very tidily. There were several rows of suits in every size, shape, and colour. There was a glass counter containing things like belts, ties, and cufflinks. There was also a shoe section with a huge stack of boxes placed against the wall. There was also a neatly arranged table with socks, doggy underwear, and handkerchiefs, all with different letters of the alphabet stitched delicately on them.

"Holy cow, just look at this store, I've never seen a place like this before, Barnaby," Cosmo said. "I've got to get me a brand-new shirt, some shoes, and a pair of those sparkly things," he carried on saying, pointing to the cufflinks. Cosmo went into the changing room with several suits. He was gone some time – Barnaby had nodded off at one point – but finally Cosmo appeared in a royal blue suit, complete with waistcoat and shiny matching shoes. He looked like a proper gentleman, so Barnaby gave him a huge paws-up sign that that was definitely the right suit! Mr Tailor packed Cosmo's purchases in a big brown paper bag; the shoes were in a box and also the cufflinks in a small presentation case. Each item had 'Tailor Made' written on it. Cosmo was delighted.

The two dogs left the shop and walked the remainder of Furever Avenue, stopping at St Bernard's Church to collect the statues that the Reverend had kept aside for Cosmo. They had had a great day but were also looking forward to going home as Barnaby's mum was arranging a BBQ that evening.

They pressed their noses against the magic dog flap and were back in Barnaby's meadow. Barnaby's mum, Neo, and Metro Politan were sitting outside on the patio with cold drinks, talking and catching up with all the family news. As time had stood still, they hadn't noticed that Barnaby and Cosmo had been away at all. The dogs made their way into the kitchen for a cool bowl of water each. Their noses were twitching – on the counter was a selection of food dishes: there were sausages, chicken, steak, and burgers. There was also baked potatoes, cheese coleslaw, and other things like tomatoes and lettuce, which they didn't particularly like the look of. However, the one thing that really stuck in Cosmo's nose was his absolute favourite thing in the whole world: cheese puffs. Cosmo adored them, so much so that they would send him into a frenzy – he'd do cartwheels to be given them. If ever Cosmo was under the weather, his dad would go out and buy him some; even if it was in the middle of the night, they always made him feel better!

"Right, you two, take yourselves outside away from the food, please," his mum said in an authoritative manner.

Both dogs did as they were told and went back outside to the garden. Cosmo's dad, Neo, had lit the barbecue. He was wearing a chef's hat and apron too. He had put up a large, long, picnic table and filled everyone's glasses with fruit punch. The late afternoon sun was still very warm, and Barnaby and Cosmo had a quick dip in the paddling pool that had been set up for them and then decided to take a short nap before dinner. Just as Cosmo was nodding off, he opened one eye and there, sitting on the top fence, was a ginger and white cat! He looked at Barnaby, who was fast asleep by now; he let out a low-pitched growl, just enough to wake him. Barnaby yawned and looked up towards the fence to see what had caught Cosmo's eye.

"Don't be bothering yourself with her, Cous, that's just Miss Catastrophe from next door," said Barnaby quite casually.

"She's staring at me, Barnaby, and she keeps looking over at the cheese puffs," Cosmo replied.

"She's not looking at those, she's looking at the salmon steaks and tuna salad," said Barnaby. Cosmo was beginning to get very annoyed; Miss Catastrophe was swishing her tail very slowly, muttering something under her breath and glaring at him. She started to walk very slowly along the fence, one eye was looking at Cosmo, the other on the cheese puffs, or so he thought. All of a sudden Miss Catastrophe jumped onto the picnic table – well, that was the end of the line for Cosmo. He let out an enormous bark and leapt up onto the other end of the table; the force of his front paws was too much for the picnic table and Miss Catastrophe was literally catapulted into the air. Everyone looked on almost like in slow motion as she flew ten feet into the air and then fell down rather quickly head first into the bowl of freshly made cheese coleslaw!

Miss Catastrophe let out a shrill, ear-shattering meow and jumped off the table, shaking her body, trying desperately to rid herself of the coleslaw that had embedded itself into her thick ginger fur. Cosmo shouted after her as she made her way over the fence, "That'll teach you, you mangy-looking feline furball!"

"Oh no, Cous," said Barnaby, "your mum and dad don't look too happy."

Cosmo's mum, Metro, had a scarlet-red face of pure embarrassment and his dad looked furious too. "OK, Cosmo," Neo shouted. "It's time to take some time out, go and upstairs and take a nap."

Cosmo was well and truly in the doghouse. Barnaby stayed where he was, not wanting to interfere or cause any more trouble. Barnaby's mum started to clean up the table; with the exception of the coleslaw, most of the other food had been spared, and everyone sat back down. They all did have to admit that it was actually quite funny! "I'll only leave him up there for a little while, he knows I'm not really angry with him. I guess he must have thought the cat was going to eat his cheese puffs," chuckled Neo.

Ten minutes later Neo went upstairs to fetch Cosmo from the doghouse. He had found him doing the exact same thing that Barnaby did when he was in trouble. He was sitting facing the wall with a sulky expression on his face. Neo gave Cosmo a handful of cheese puffs and he followed him downstairs. Barnaby wagged his tail, so pleased to see his cousin. The two dogs settled in front of the TV, leaving the humans to enjoy the rest of their evening. It had been such an eventful day that both dogs dropped off to sleep halfway through their favourite show called *Off the Leash*.

Barnaby would dream his usual dream but also he would look forward to another day in Goldenwood; who knew what he would do there next!

BARNABY MAKES A TV APPEARANCE

Barnaby woke from his usual dream to the sound of the postman pushing the mail through the letterbox downstairs. He was feeling a little nervous and had butterflies in his tummy. He didn't know how they got there as he didn't remember eating them! He made his way downstairs, straight into the kitchen where the radio was playing yet another favourite song by a group called The Village Dogs. He cheerily sang along. The reason he was feeling nervous was because today he was going to appear on TV.

Apart from being a good chess player, Barnaby was also very good at general knowledge. He had applied several weeks ago to be on the quiz show *Million Dollar Dawgie*. He had already been up to the Goldenwood Studios for an audition and now they wanted him to be on the show for real. Barnaby only managed an abnormally small breakfast due to his nervousness; he hoped he wouldn't have to keep running to the little dogs room like when he and Cosmo finally found their way out of the maze! Barnaby walked up his meadow, spotting Miss Catastrophe out of the corner of his eye, he called over to her, "Lovely perfume, Miss Catastrophe, is it called Eau de'Coleslaw?" She scowled at Barnaby, muttering something under her breath like she always did, then jumped back over to her garden.

Barnaby pushed open the door of the magic dog flap and through the other side to Goldenwood. He didn't take the usual route down Furever Avenue; he took a left turn instead into Waggatail Way, as this was the quickest way to the Goldenwood Studios. There weren't any shops on the way but there were larger houses that were occupied by some of the more famous residents of Goldenwood. There were also stars carved into the pavement with the names of famous dogs on them. Barnaby stopped at the gates of the entrance to the Goldenwood Studios – he was feeling more nervous than ever before in his life. A large dog appeared who was of the German Shepherd dog kind. He took Barnaby's name and opened the big, tall gates and told him to make his way into the reception area.

Inside there a few other dogs who all looked just as nervous as Barnaby did. Five minutes later a lady dog of the Dalmatian dog kind came out and introduced herself as Daphne, the makeup and wardrobe assistant. He immediately thought that she needed to go and visit Dr Sore-Paw, as she had terrible black spots all over her. Barnaby followed her into the dressing room, where she brushed his hair and even powdered his nose. He didn't want to change into one of the outfits they suggested, so he stayed in his comfortable cotton trousers and shirt. He could hear the audience cheering as one of the announcers warmed them up. He made one last trip to the little dogs' room, as he would shortly be introduced to the host of the show, Nathaniel Spaniel. A couple of minutes later the dressing room door opened and in walked Nathaniel. Barnaby immediately recognised him. He was shorter than Barnaby had imagined and of the Spaniel dog kind. He was wearing a white suit and a power blue shirt with a pink tie and when he smiled you could see his huge, gleaming white teeth. Barnaby laughed, as he thought that the makeup assistant had rather over-powdered Nathaniel's nose. He also was wearing a very heavy doggy aftershave that made Barnaby's eyes water!

The moment had arrived when it was Barnaby's turn to take the hot seat, he was worried about the hot seat because he didn't want it to burn his beautiful fluffy behind! The audience cheered as the announcer said, "Welcome to *Million Dollar Dawgie* and here is your host, Mr Nathaniel Spaniel!" Barnaby was then introduced as the next contestant and he made his way to the hot seat; suddenly he felt his nerves disappear and his heart stopped pounding so hard. He sat down as the audience applauded. Nathaniel then explained the rules of the game. "Welcome, Barnaby, as you know you will be asked ten questions, you will also have a lifeline of phoning a friend for help. If you answer all ten questions correctly, you will become our next Million Dollar Dawgie!"

The lights dimmed in the studio and Nathaniel read the first question out: "Question one: in which country does the Golden Retriever originally come from?"

Easy, thought Barnaby, replying with the answer, "Scotland."

"Question two: in which county in the human land of England is the town of Barking?"

Barnaby knew this one too! "Essex," he replied.

"Question three: which group sang 'Who Let the Dogs Out'?"

This is easy, thought Barnaby. "The correct answer is the Baha Men," he replied.

"Question four, Barnaby, is a bit harder," said Nathaniel. "What is the official state flower of North Carolina?"

"Hmm," said Barnaby. "I think it's called the flowering dogwood, but I'd like to phone my friend Roxy, please, Nathaniel." Roxy lived in North Carolina across the big pond in America. Roxy was a blonde Golden Retriever like Barnaby. She was quite stocky, too, but so very pretty; Barnaby had a picture of her on his bedside table. Roxy had rescued her mum and dad some years ago, so she was the new boss of the house. She had her parents and little brother Remy firmly under her paw. Remy was a redhead, but not like CC for Short; he was also a Golden Retriever. Roxy would tease her brother about being frightened to use the dog flap at home, calling him a 'Scaredy-Dog'. She also knew everything there was to know about flowers, as she had a huge garden and her mum had planted lots of different kinds and Roxy had learned all their names off by heart. Barnaby still wanted to check the answer anyway, as he didn't want to take chance of losing 400,000 dawgie dollars.

Nathaniel lifted the phone and dialled Roxy's number; she picked up the phone almost straightaway. Nathaniel explained who he was and that Barnaby was in the hot seat and he asked her the question. "Flowering dogwood, 100% certain," Roxy said in a soft American accent. The audience clapped and cheered. Barnaby was so excited – he was nearly halfway through and so far he'd got all the questions right.

"Question five: in the film *The Incredible Journey*, what are the names of the two dogs?"

Another easy one, Barnaby thought confidently. "The answer is Shadow and Chance," replied Barnaby.

"Absolutely correct," said Nathaniel. "Question six: what kind of dog has webbed feet?"

"I know the answer to this too," said Barnaby. "It's the Newfoundland!"

"Correct again," said Nathaniel. "Question seven: in the human royal family, what was the name of Queen Elizabeth the Second's first Corgi?"

Barnaby thought carefully about this one – he didn't have his lifeline left so he'd have to be sure of the answer. Then, quick as a flash, it came to him. "The answer is Susan!" Barnaby exclaimed.

"Correct," replied Nathaniel. "Question eight: what is the name of the TV show featuring sheep dogs and trials in the human world?"

Barnaby knew this too, as he watched it often. "The answer is *One Man and His Dog*," he replied.

"Correct again, Barnaby," said Nathaniel. "Question nine: name two kinds of dog that are completely hairless."

"Difficult question," said Barnaby, "but I know the names of two – they are Chinese Crested and Peruvian Hairless."

Nathaniel looked Barnaby right in the eyes and said, "Correct! Now, Barnaby, here is the final question. Question ten: what was the name of the world's tallest dog, who sadly passed away in 2014?"

Barnaby knew this – he couldn't believe it, his cousin Cosmo had mentioned it when he was talking about Pastry the Goldenwood Great Dane, and that this particular dog was from Michigan in America, just like Cosmo. "The answer is Zeus," he said. The studio fell silent; you could have heard a hairball drop.

"Barnaby," said Nathaniel, "you've just won one million dawgie dollars, congratulations!"

The audience went wild – it sounded like every dog was howling with sheer delight and happiness for Barnaby. Barnaby stood up and cleared his throat, ready to say a few words. He knew that he wouldn't be able to keep the money, as it wasn't worth anything in the human world. He had often thought what he would do if he won, and he had decided that he would donate the money to the Reverend Dawg-Collar's various good causes. They would be able to help house all the homeless doggies, buy toys, endless food, and treats to last a lifetime. Barnaby did, however, insist on one thing that he personally thought all the residents of Goldenwood would enjoy. He wanted to create a big park with a large outdoor swimming pool and a smaller one for all the young puppies. Barnaby thanked the audience and Nathaniel for having him on the show and proceeded to tell them all of his plans. The audience gasped and cheered and howled even louder than before. Barnaby blushed with both delight and embarrassment – he thought that he might have to rush to the little dogs' room again at one point!

An aftershow party had been arranged and every dog was invited. Barnaby made a quick trip to the little dogs' room to freshen up and comb his hair. He felt rather proud of himself. He took out his iBone and sent a fleamail to Roxy, thanking her for helping him and to tell her about his big win. He wished he could take some of his winnings into the human world so that he go and visit her. Barnaby made his way into the function room, where there was a table filled with various treats and snacks. There were several dogs dressed in smart suits carrying trays full of every drink you could imagine, also cheese and miniature sausages on cocktail sticks. They had even managed to fill a few glasses with holy water for the Reverend

Dawg-Collar and his family to enjoy. Nathaniel had attracted the attention of several lady dogs, including Daphne the hair and wardrobe assistant that Barnaby had seen earlier. It turned out that Daphne Foreclaw was the rescued daughter of the Foreclaw-Kennelworths; they had found her roaming the streets cold and hungry when her dog-mother had tragically passed away. She was now as much a part of the family as their own pups. Nathaniel was loving all the attention – it seemed that he had what Barnaby's mum would call a reputation. Nathaniel was also signing pawtographs and framed pictures of himself for everyone as a keepsake of remembering the day.

A couple of hours later, Barnaby said his goodbyes and made his way back down Waggatail Way. He stopped off at the big field that would eventually become the new park and swimming centre. Some pups were playing on the old slides and sand pits that had been there for years. He hoped that the new park would be enjoyed by all the Goldenwood dogs – there would be no entrance fee, but you could make a donation and also receive a free ticket entitling you to never-ending ice-cream.

Barnaby made a quick detour down Furever Avenue, he wanted to call in at Goldenwoods Glorious Gift Shop to buy a present for Roxy. Gloria Barker was of the Collie dog kind; she was quite old with a grey muzzle and always wore a flowery apron. She was very friendly and proud of her shop. Gloria had opened it a couple of years back after retiring from her job at the farm where she took care of the sheep. The shop sold so many treasures of every kind; they also had regular toys and accessories too. Barnaby particularly liked the bouncing musical tennis balls and the five feet tall stuffed flamingo! After browsing the shelves for some time, he decided on a wooden keepsake box; when you lifted the lid it played a tune and up popped a dancing doggy. The outside of the box was also painted with pictures of red roses and heart-shaped paw prints. Barnaby knew that Roxy would love it. He had Gloria gift wrap it, also enclosing a lock of hair and finishing it off with a pink ribbon. Barnaby wrote a special little card out saying, "To dear Roxy, thank you for your help, I hope you like the gift, I think you are so very beautiful, love from your friend, Barnaby x."

Barnaby wanted to mail Roxy's present straight away, so he made his way to the Goldenwood

Post Office. The postmaster, whose name was Reg D'elivery, was of the Corgi dog kind. He wasn't very tall and was sitting on an elevated chair. He took Barnaby's package and put it on the weighing scale – he then placed his paw pad in something that resembled ink and heavily pressed on the top right-hand side of the package to imprint the postage mark. Of course Goldenwood mail was kept secret from the human world, but Roxy would find it safely delivered in the secret place they had spoken about in the past.

Barnaby began to feel tired; it had been a long day. He made his way back up Furever Avenue. Major Headline, who owned the Newsagent's Shop, was waving a copy of the evening paper. Major was of the Airedale dog kind; retired many years ago, he was once an Army Major Service Dog. He had even been locked up in a dog prisoner of war camp. He told many stories of his awful experiences – he was indeed very courageous and still proudly wore his medals on his jacket. Barnaby was on the front cover of the paper. He had never made the headlines before, so he bought a copy from Major and sat down at the Bark and Ride to stop and read it. A few dogs walked past, recognising Barnaby and congratulating him. He felt tremendously proud – he was glad he had answered all the questions right but even prouder that he could help others in the Goldenwood community.

He finally reached the magic dog flap and pushed his way through. As always everything was just as he had left it. It was quiet and even Miss Catastrophe seemed to have learned her lesson and was nowhere to be seen. He picked up a slipper that he had safely buried a few days ago and went into the house. Mum was watching a cookery show and writing down recipes whilst drinking tea. He climbed on the sofa beside her, hooking his paws over her knees. "Hello, Barn," she said affectionately, kissing him on his head. "I do so love you," she continued. Barnaby gulped – he loved her too and he wished she could hear him say it back, but of course he was back home now. He swished his tail in approval and nodded off to sleep. Tomorrow was another day and another adventure.

STORY FIVE

THE GOLDENWOOD
GAMES!

Barnaby woke up from his usual dream and looked at his alarm clock – it was 8am. He had slept in, which was most unusual for him considering it was a weekday. His bedroom door was open, so he assumed that his mum had looked in on him earlier but he had still been fast asleep. He stretched his body and shook his coat off, making his way downstairs, he heard the radio playing as usual. The song this morning was another good one.

He finished his breakfast and then did a cute little rubby face thing along the living room couch and then went to the garden for a roll on the damp grass. It was autumn now, but it was still warm during the day. This was Barnaby's favourite season, as he loved the crisp mornings and the feel of the fall leaves on his paws. He was excited about the day ahead, as he was attending the Goldenwood Games. It was like a dog version of the human Olympic Games, but it was held every year rather than every four. Pushing his nose through the magic dog flap, he looked for Bert the Town Crier. Bert was nowhere to be seen; Barnaby then remembered that Bert was taking place in the shot put event at the games. He was a Bulldog, of course, and very strong. Barnaby thought that he had a good chance of winning a gold medal.

Making his way down Furever Avenue, there were posters advertising the games and flags flying high, gently blowing in the wind. He turned right at the corner of the Post Office building, making his way through Goldenwood Park and up to the stadium where all the sporting events were taking place. The stadium had only been built a couple of years ago and all sorts of events had taken place since, such as football, rugby and cricket competitions. He gave his day ticket to the attendant and bought a copy of the programme. Glancing down, he made a mental note of the events he wanted to watch. He had to make sure to meet Spirit on the dot of noon as CC for Short was playing tennis and he had wanted to watch her – she was through to the final!

He decided that he would go and watch the dock diving competition first, and then go to watch CC for Short, and after lunch watch Bert in his shot put competition. He then wanted to go and see the indoor tenpin bowling and, if he had time, maybe the running event. Barnaby made his way to the river, picking up a double scoop vanilla ice-cream cone on the way. His friend Theo was competing, who was of the Newfoundland dog kind. He had webbed feet – a lot of dogs were shocked at his dock diving abilities as he was extremely large and very heavily set, but he just took to it like a duck to water! Theo was a teacher by day normally; his full name was Theory Lesson. He taught at the Goldenwood School and he was liked by his pupils and colleagues as he was very knowledgeable but had a way of explaining things with a marvellous sense of humour that made it easier for his students to understand.

Barnaby finished his ice-cream and took his seat at the river's edge. Theo was next up. He looked very confident and showed no sign of nerves. He took a long run up the dock, launching himself into the air, his body stretched out like an aeroplane taking off. There was a huge splash and then an unusual silence while the judges took the measurements. Barnaby thought that Theo must have easily cleared fifteen feet. The audience clapped and cheered. *Wow, what an achievement*, thought Barnaby. That had to be a world record, but he still had to wait for all the scores to come in. There were two other competitors left, the first being Tiny Dancer – she was a Golden Retriever too but much more slender than Barnaby; her coat was slightly darker and she was tall for her breed. Tiny made an impressive dive and Barnaby couldn't see whether it was longer than Theo's, but it must be very close. Now it was the final competitor's turn. Hope Springs was a Springer Spaniel. She was medium height, very lean and incredibly bouncy. Her dive was fantastic – now Barnaby was really worried! After what seemed at least half an hour – but was actually only a few minutes – the judge stood up and read out the scores. "Taking the bronze medal, with 15.8 feet, is Tiny Dancer," he said in a forthright manner. "The silver medal, with 16.5 feet, is Hope Springs, and in first place, taking the gold medal with a very impressive 16.8 feet, is Theory Lesson!" The crowd cheered and clapped with joy for all the competitors. All three dogs took to the podium and received their medals. *How magnificent,* thought Barnaby. He also took a second look at the silver and bronze medal winners again, as they were both very pretty dogs whom he had never seen before but hoped he would see again!

Barnaby looked at his watch – it was ten to twelve and he had to meet Spirit soon. He made his way back to the main stadium and round to the tennis courts. Spirit was waiting at the entrance and they made their way to their seats. The players hadn't arrived on court yet, it was hot, and Barnaby was very appreciative that Spirit had bought them both some fruit juice. Both dogs were also wearing baseball caps too, and sunglasses to shield them from the heat and glare. CC for Short and her opponent were making their way to the court – she was up against Priscilla Pettyclaw, who was of the Irish Wolfhound dog kind. She was extremely tall and muscular, and held the current title. CC was tall and very agile but looked small by comparison. Both dogs were experienced players, having played in the junior tournaments since they were pups.

Priscilla won the first set. Spirit looked very nervous, but he knew CC was good enough to beat her. As if she had read his mind, CC won three points, then a game; she had to win one more game to draw one set each. The ball flew backwards and forwards, both players leaping into the air and hitting it with all their might. CC won the next game, but Priscilla's hit back made it two-all, so they were level. Spirit and Barnaby leant forward in their seats – this final game would be the decider. Priscilla was three points up. *Oh no*, thought Barnaby, *it's match point*. CC levelled off and then got the advantage – it was now match point to her! Spirit could hardly watch, then all of a sudden, she got the point. CC for Short had won. The umpire shouted out the words, "Game, set, match, Miss Redcoat!" CC looked delighted she blew a kiss to the audience, Spirit thought it was for him, so he blushed with embarrassment. Barnaby and Spirit left their seats. Spirit decided to wait for CC; she was signing pawtographs, but he wanted to see her and congratulate her and then take her for lunch.

Next Barnaby made his way to the shot put contest. He hoped he wasn't too late to see Bert in action – it was a five-minute walk to the back field where it was being held. Barnaby arrived just as Bert was taking his turn. He could see the strength in Bert's paws and put this down to the fact that as he was the town crier and that he was always using the muscles in his arm to ring his handbell. Barnaby didn't even think he could even lift the shot, let alone throw it – he had never been particularly athletic. Bert was up against the McDawgle brothers: they were identical triplets called Angus, Tavish and Jock, and were of the Scottish Terrier dog kind. They weren't particularly big or muscular, but rumour had it that they were tough. They also had a reputation for being very unfriendly; this showed in their faces which were always frowning.

Fortunately for Bert, first up was Angus. Angus had a terrible fear of insects but wasps in particular. Just as he was about to throw the shot, an enormous one landed on his paw. Angus tossed the shot into the air, howling with fear at the top of his voice. He ran off into the crowd, followed closely by the wasp, the audience watching and chuckling from the sidelines. Barnaby laughed so hard he felt his tummy go into a knot. *One down, two to go*, he thought. Next up was Jock – he threw well but not as good as Bert. Tavish stepped forward for his turn. He had a very egotistical look on his face like he was certain to win – he even had the nerve to turn around and say, "This is how it's really done!" What Tavish didn't realise was that one of his shoelaces had come undone and as he picked up the shot and threw it, he fell head first in a heap! Just like his brother Angus, Tavish ran out the field in total embarrassment – the laughter from the audience was even louder than when Angus had ran away. Barnaby was certain that Bert must be the winner, as Jock's throw was a very weak effort. The judge stepped forward and announced the winner – of course it was Bert! Barnaby was thrilled. *Three in a row*, he thought. First Theo, then CC for Short and now Bert had all achieved gold medals.

It was 1.30pm now. Barnaby grabbed a quick hotdog (of the edible kind) with lashings of ketchup and made his way to the tenpin indoor bowling alley. Tenpin bowling had never been done before at the games, only outdoor bowling on a green. It was popular in Goldenwood, though, and a regular treat for most families at the weekend. Another of Barnaby's friends was competing. Jacob Bowler-Skittle was of the Basset dog kind. He was very short with a long body and ears to match. Barnaby was sat high up, looking down at the alley from the observation area while Jacob was putting on his special bowling shoes. Another contender was about to take his turn. Barnaby wasn't familiar with this particular dog, but he remembered seeing him playing darts at the pub when Cosmo was visiting. It turned out it was Major's grandson from the Newsagent's Shop; he was a confident bowler but Barnaby thought he missed a few good opportunities and should have scored better. The dog who really was the one to watch was Franz Bratwurst, who was of the Rottweiler dog kind. Originally from Germany, he had lived in Goldenwood for about four years after he sadly lost his humans. He still had a heavy accent and, although he looked fierce and strong, he was known as a gentle giant. He was a fantastic bowler.

Jacob was next – he stood with his bowling ball gripped tightly in his left paw, his claws tucked into the holes on either side. He swung his paw back and forth and then, with an almighty force, he sent the ball flying down the alley! "Yes," he shouted at having a direct hit. He repeated the process several times, his score increasing rapidly.

Last up was Franz, who said something in German and started swaying from side to side, his bowling shoes squeaking on the newly polished floor. It was almost like a ritual that he performed. He took his ball in his paw and flung his arm back and forth like Jacob but much faster. Franz also did something that was very unique to his style of the game – he always took a good run up to the lane before letting the ball go. There was a deadly silence as Franz manoeuvred himself into position. He stepped back about twenty feet and all of a sudden flew towards the lane, his ball clasped like a vice in his paw. It was then that it all went terribly wrong, Barnaby couldn't see exactly what happened, whether Franz slipped on the floor causing him to lose his balance or if his run up was just too enthusiastic. Rather than just the ball flying up the lane, Franz went hurtling down it too! He was going at such a speed that there was no way he could stop himself. Approaching the skittles, he let the ball go and put both of his front paws up to shield his face. There was an almighty crash as Franz disappeared behind the skittles! The machine then automatically reset itself, but Franz was nowhere to be seen. Fortunately, Dr Sore-Paw was in the audience and he rushed to help. After about ten minutes Franz appeared, looking somewhat confused and embarrassed. Feeling a little guilty about even thinking this, Barnaby was happy that this meant that Jacob would be awarded the gold medal. *Four down, one to go!* he said to himself.

Barnaby just had time to make it to the athletics track to watch his final chosen event of the day. He was going to watch his friend Gatsby in the five-hundred-metre race. Gatsby Houndsman-Hunter was of the Greyhound dog kind. He was tall, very slender and extremely fast. He loved his food and drink but never gained much weight. He was a happy chappy who enjoyed racing for the fun of it and had never been forced to run competitively, unlike some Greyhounds in the human world. He was also the patron of the GGRA – the Goldenwood Greyhound Rescue Association. His friends gave him the nickname of 'The Great Gatsby'! Barnaby took his seat; the dogs were lined up at the start of the track and waited for the signal to begin the race. As quick as a flash, the dogs were off – they were all running so fast you could barely make out their bodies. Barnaby had no idea who was in the lead, the race was over so quickly. The winner would be announced by the commentator shortly. It was declared a photo finish between Gatsby and Sherlock. Sherlock Homes owned a kennel building business and was friends with Gatsby and Barnaby, so it would be difficult not to be happy whoever won, really, but he had known Gatsby the longest, though, so his loyalty did lean slightly with him. The commentator then called out the winner – it was Gatsby! "Yes," shouted Barnaby. "Five in a row: Theo, CC for Short, Bert, Jacob and Gatsby!"

Barnaby had enjoyed the day so much; he had taken lots of photos and video footage on his iBone and would fleamail them to his friends later. He had never laughed so much, apart from maybe the time when he was walking his mum and he dragged her into a hedge, causing her major embarrassment as a bus-load of people witnessed the whole thing!

He made his way back through Goldenwood Park and then up Furever Avenue. Nudging the magic dog flap, he stepped back into his meadow.

Just as before, time had stood still – the washing was on the line along with some of Barnaby's stuffies. Barnaby sat down on the patio, resting his chin on the cool paving stones. He must have nodded off, because he didn't even hear his mum come home from shopping. There would be another adventure to come soon in the wonderful world of Goldenwood!

STORY SIX

CHRISTMAS IN GOLDENWOOD!

Barnaby awoke from his usual dream to the sound of sleigh bells – at least that's what he thought he heard, anyway. He'd forgotten he'd changed the fleamail alert sound on his iBone! It was three days before Christmas and he was getting very excited. Barnaby loved everything about Christmas: he loved presents, the decorations and tree, singing carols, and seeing old friends, but most of all, he loved the food. He was looking forward to today, as he was going to Goldenwood for some early Christmas celebrations.

Barnaby made his way downstairs. Stepping into the lounge, his eyes focused on the Christmas tree. There were still no presents underneath; he had heard his mum saying something to his dad about them: "Barnaby will open them if we put them under before Christmas Day," she had said forcefully. He had written a letter to Santa Paws already in anticipation of the big day. In his best paw-writing he wrote:

Dear Santa Paws,

Please could I have the following for Christmas:

1. *A new stuffed animal (one of those five-feet-tall pink flamingos).*
2. *A red bandana.*
3. *A treat selection box.*

I've been very good for most of the year, just ask my friends in Goldenwood. I do, however, apologise for the following:

I should NOT have rolled in that horse manure (three times).

I should NOT have stolen and then eaten that whole cheese pizza that gave me the most shocking wind.

I should NOT have ripped the stuffing out of one of my favourite toys, Mr Bun the Baker Man.

I really should NOT have gone running to the front door with Mum's underwear in my mouth.

There were a few other mishaps over the year, but you're a very busy man, so I'll not tell you about them. I hope you understand, Santa.

Paws sincerely,
Barnaby Dyson xxx

He carried on into the kitchen; he couldn't smell anything cooking, but he could hear a Christmas favourite playing on the radio, Barnaby sang along. Mum looked up from what she was doing and said, "There you are, Barn, I have to go to the supermarket, I'll take you for a walk when I get home, I'll leave the back door open but the gate locked," looking at Barnaby as if he understood every word! Of course, he understood, plus he was going to Goldenwood and was way too excited to worry about not getting his morning walk on time.

Barnaby walked up his meadow; the grass was frosty, but he still couldn't resist having a quick roll. Miss Catastrophe wasn't around, indeed she hadn't ventured anywhere near the garden or even sat on the fence since the coleslaw incident. He had felt a little bit bad for her at one point, but she had been mean to him in the past, so he quickly put those thoughts out his head. Barnaby pressed his nose against the magic dog flap, but it didn't open at first. *My nose must be cold*, he thought, *I'll just rub it along the grass a bit more to warm it up.* He tried again and this time it opened! Bert was stood at the other side – he was wearing his red tunic as usual but with some holly tucked into his button holes, and a sprig of mistletoe in his hat where his feather usually was; he looked very festive.

Barnaby turned left and made his way down the familiar route of Furever Avenue. Walking past St Bernard's Church, he smiled at the nativity scene outside the entrance – there were models of a mother and father dog and their pup in the manger. He would be attending the Christmas Carol service later on. Furever Avenue was beautifully decorated with twinkling lights, talking Santas and real Christmas trees on every corner – it looked like a Christmas film set. All the shops were fabulously decorated too! There was much excitement, as all the shop owners were having a Christmas decoration competition. He and his friends Jacob and Gatsby had been asked to judge it.

Barnaby was to meet Jacob and Gatsby for lunch at The Full Bowl Pub. He had invited Spirit too, but he was lucky enough to be going on a trip to Lapland for Christmas with his human family. First on Barnaby's agenda, however, was a trip to the Goldenwood Theatre to see the Goldenwood Players perform the pantomime *Cinderella*. Tiny Dancer had been given the part of Cinderella – Barnaby remembered her from the dock diving event at the Goldenwood Games, but he still hadn't had the opportunity of meeting her. *Maybe next year*, he thought. Dut-Chess and Luci-Fur were playing the parts of the ugly sisters! The ladies were getting along so much better now and had managed to reconcile their differences. Luci had even become actively involved with the charities that the Reverend Dawg-Collar took care of too. She also volunteered at the Goldenwood Library three times a week, often helping the younger pups out with their reading.

Barnaby took his seat at the theatre – it was full of families with their young pups, most of which were happily munching on pupcorn snacks and other treats. The curtain went up and what followed could only be best described as a production full of belly-aching laughter and other shenanigans. There were characters flying in the air, singing pantomime horses and dogs falling through trap doors. Tiny, Dut-Chess, and Luci performed magnificently. Major Headline, who had produced the show, had done a wonderful job. The crowd cheered for a good five minutes at the end as the cast took their final bows. Outside in the foyer, Santa Paws was sitting waiting to greet all the young puppies, who were so very excited to see him. They each got their photo taken with him and a present too. Barnaby couldn't help think, though, that Santa looked very much like Henry Foreclaw-Kennelworth. Maybe his eyes were deceiving him or maybe they weren't. Santa winked at Barnaby as he walked past as if to say, you know it's me, Barnaby, but don't tell the pups!

Barnaby made his way to The Full Bowl Pub to meet Jacob and Gatsby. He hadn't seen either of them since they had won their medals at the Goldenwood Games. Inside, the pub was festively decorated. There was a huge tree in the corner with twinkling lights and brightly coloured baubles. Barnaby spotted his friends waiting at a table overlooking the garden. They were having a carvery lunch, which all three dogs were looking forward to tremendously. They ordered some drinks and made their way to the counter to select their lunches. There were huge platters of roast turkey, beef, pork, chicken, and goose, plus side dishes of chipolata sausages wrapped in bacon, chestnut stuffing, Yorkshire puddings, roast potatoes, vegetables, and, last but not least, lashings of gravy. Christmas carols were playing in the background and Barnaby had a marvellous feeling of contentment, particularly in his stomach. After lunch, the three dogs went back into the main lounge for another drink and a catch-up chat, allowing their meals to digest! They agreed to meet at the bottom of Furever Avenue at four o'clock sharp to judge the decoration competition.

Next he had agreed to meet Dilly and Dally at the Goldenwood Ice Rink. Barnaby had always wanted to learn to skate properly. Spirit and CC for Short were fabulous skaters and put Barnaby to shame. He always felt so silly because he could hardly stand on the ice, never mind skate. Dilly and Dally had taught many dogs in the past and were convinced that they could definitely help Barnaby pick it up. He made his way down Furcoat Drive to the ice rink. Dilly and Dally were waiting for him in the foyer, their ice-skating boots hanging around their necks. They had also kindly brought a pair for Barnaby which they had borrowed from Dilly's friend, who was also a golden retriever – fortunately they were the same paw size!

Out on the ice it was quite chilly and there was music playing in the background. Several dogs were skating, all going in one direction in time with the music. Everyone looked so Christmassy, wearing red outfits and tinsel in their hair. Barnaby suddenly felt very nervous – he hoped he didn't have to go to the little dogs' room. Dilly and Dally stood either side of him, holding a paw each to steady him. After a few falls on his behind, he eventually started moving slowly in time to the music. He felt marvellous; Dilly and Dally then let go of his paws to give him a go at skating unaided. He did – he was skating properly all by himself and he didn't fall once. Dilly and Dally cheered him on from the sidelines. After several minutes, Barnaby very carefully made his way over to join them. He was so relieved to be holding on to the barrier.

"You did great!" exclaimed Dilly and Dally in unison.

"I feel rather stiff, and I don't think I'll ever be a champion, but thank you both for helping me," replied Barnaby. At least now he could join Spirit and CC for Short. He did think afterwards, though, that he would probably make his excuses if he was asked to go again, as skating really wasn't his thing. He considered himself more of an academic dog who preferred doing activities sitting down! Barnaby thanked the ladies again and took off his boots. His paws were stiff and aching. He couldn't wait to get to St Bernard's Church for the carol service and have a well-deserved sit down, but he still had to meet Jacob and Gatsby for the competition judging – at least he had burned off his lunch, though!

Barnaby made his way down Furcoat Drive and then into Furever Avenue. There were crowds forming all along the Avenue in anticipation of the competition. It had been a very difficult decision, as all the shops looked fabulous. However, the one that really stood out was Mr Chip-Olatas Butcher's Shop. He had a singing turkey outside, and in the window there were three wise dogs carrying trays of meat and poultry. There were twinkling lights around the windows and a large pig dressed in a Santa suit that oinked when you walked past it. There was also a Mother Hen festively dressed with a coin slot in her apron. The young pups adored this, as when they inserted the coin, the hen said the words, "Have an eggscellent Christmas," and then went on to lay an egg-shaped dog treat. Barnaby, Jacob, and Gatsby read out the winner in unison, while the crowd cheered and clapped. Everyone was thrilled for Chip; he was a very worthy winner.

Barnaby could hear the church bells ringing out. The Reverend and Mrs Dawg-Collar were waiting outside to greet their parishioners. Barnaby took a pew, grateful to be sitting down. The Reverend addressed the congregation and the service began. They sang a variety of carols, including some modern-day ones. At one point, some dogs were dancing in the aisles, even the Reverend was swinging his hips and raising his paws in the air – it was a wonderful service! After a prayer and a final rousing chorus of 'O Come All Ye Faithful', the service drew to a close. Barnaby went to light a candle for all the dogs and humans that were no longer of this earth. He hoped they would all be celebrating together in heaven too this Christmas.

The congregation made their way outside. Barnaby was taken by surprise when Priscilla Petty-Claw grabbed him and pulled him under the mistletoe for a sneaky kiss – he blushed with embarrassment! Barnaby made a quick exit, as he knew that she, just like Nathaniel Spaniel, had a bit of a reputation. He knew that his mum would tell him to definitely stay away from dogs like that.

Making his way up the rest of Furever Avenue, he pushed his nose against the magic dog flap and back into his meadow. Just as always, everything was as he had left it. Time, of course, had stood still, and his mum wasn't back from shopping. *Good*, he thought. He definitely needed a nap. He was so tired that he wasn't even tempted to steal the plate of mince pies and mulled wine that were mistakenly left on the kitchen table.

He drifted off to sleep. Soon Christmas would be here and a New Year, too. This would bring so many new adventures and memories that made him the original Goldenwood Barnaby!

Matador

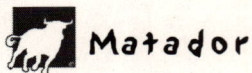

For exclusive discounts on Matador titles,
sign up to our occasional newsletter at
troubador.co.uk/bookshop